DEDICATION

For the ones who've ever listened to the wind through
the barn slats,
stood still in the silence,
or felt the weight of memories in a place time forgot.

To my Daddy—whose hands taught me work, whose
love taught me strength,
and whose spirit still rides the pasture with me.

To my family—blood and chosen—thank you for your
love, laughter, and support,
even when the road was crooked and the dust was
thick.

And to the ones reading this:
May you find pieces of yourself tucked between these
pages,
and may you always trust what your heart already
knows.

With all my love,
Janet McClain Canady

Chapter 1 - Gravel Roads and Ghosts

Janna Rae Calhoun hadn't set foot on that pasture in near twenty years, but somehow, her boots still knew where to land. The old driveway kicked up more dust than welcome, and her truck door creaked louder than her knees when she stepped out. She stood there for a second, just breathin' it in—pine, hay, and the faint scent of rusted regrets.

The pasture stretched out ahead of her, same as it always had. Wide, quiet, and stubborn. Like it was waitin' on her to apologize.

She didn't. Not yet.

Behind her, the house slumped into the earth like it had given up waitin'. One shutter dangled, and the porch steps looked like they'd bite her if she stepped wrong. But it was home. Or had been. Or might be again—Lord only knew.

A crow cawed from the fence post like it had somethin' to say about all this.

"Well," Janna muttered, "I didn't ask for commentary."

She grabbed her overnight bag, slung it over her shoulder, and stepped toward the porch. The gravel crunched like old bones under her boots. Every step was a memory she wasn't ready for.

She came back to settle a few things. Maybe the past. Maybe herself. Maybe both.

And somewhere out in that field, in the grass grown high and wild, was the truth she'd buried before she ever left.

Chapter 2 - The Will and the Way Home

Janna Rae hated paperwork almost as much as she hated funerals. And today, she was neck-deep in both.

She sat at the rickety kitchen table in Birdie's house, staring at a manila envelope like it might bite her. Whit Montgomery—clean-cut, over starched, and smellin' like aftershave and courtroom money—stood at the counter thumbing through a folder like he had all the time in the world.

"This is just formality," he said, flipping a page. "Birdie's estate isn't large, but there are… conditions."

Janna narrowed her eyes. "Conditions? This ain't some game show, Mr. Montgomery. She owned a house, a pasture, and three goats that ain't been seen in six months."

He looked up, amused. "Actually, the goats are in the neighbor's yard. Darlene Ferguson called my office twice about it."

Of course she did.

He cleared his throat and held up a page.

"Per Birdie Calhoun's will, in order to take full ownership of the home and land, you must reside on the property for a period of **ninety consecutive days.** No selling, no leasing, no leavin'. After ninety days, it's yours—free and clear."

Janna blinked. "I gotta live here? For three months?"

"Correct."

She looked around the kitchen—peeling linoleum, a fridge that wheezed like a dying mule, and the ghost of a woman who once ruled this house with an iron skillet and a soft heart.

"You're kidding."

Whit shrugged. "She was very specific. Said you needed time with the land. That it knew things you didn't."

Janna opened her mouth to argue—but stopped.

That sounded *exactly* like Birdie.

Still, it wasn't just the clause that rattled her. It was the other envelope. The one Whit slid across the table a few minutes ago. Smaller. Handwritten. Her name on the front in Birdie's loopy cursive.

Janna Rae — For your eyes only.

It sat in front of her like a coiled snake.

"You said she gave this to you before she passed?" Janna asked.

Whit nodded. "Told me not to open it. Just to deliver it… after I read you the will."

The room felt suddenly smaller. Heavier. Janna could hear her own heartbeat over the tick of the wall clock.

She picked it up slowly, thumbing the seal.

"I'll leave you to it," Whit said, gathering his briefcase. "You've got ninety days to decide what comes next."

She didn't answer. She couldn't.

Not yet.

She waited for his car to roll down the gravel road before peeling the envelope open with trembling fingers.

Inside was a single sheet of folded paper. And the words written in Birdie's hand?

"I wasn't always honest with you, baby girl. But the truth lives in the pasture. Start where your mama ended."

Chapter 3 - Boots on Borrowed Ground

The sun had just started its slow climb when Janna Rae stepped off the porch and into the dew-soaked grass, her boots swallowing a soft squish that made her wince. The pasture stretched wide in front of her, overgrown, tangled, and wild — just like her thoughts.

She hadn't slept much. That letter from Birdie had kept her up most of the night, turning over the words like stones in her hand.

"Start where your mama ended."

Problem was… Janna didn't *know* where her mama ended.

Hell, she barely remembered where she *started*.

All she knew was that her mama, **Maylene Calhoun**, packed up and left one night when Janna was just nine years old. No note. No goodbye. No answer ever given — just Birdie standing at the sink the next morning, scrubbin' dishes with a vengeance and sayin', "Your mama's gone and that's that."

And now, decades later, Birdie was gone too — but apparently not done talkin'.

Janna hiked up the hill toward the back of the pasture, past the rusted swing that used to creak her to sleep on summer evenings. Past the old tool shed, halfcollapsed, still holdin' tight to the smell of oil and secrets. She found herself drifting toward the one place she hadn't set foot in since she was a teenager — the **old well house**.

Its tin roof was bent and jagged, like a hat stomped too many times. Vines crept up its side, claiming it slow. But the door opened easy, and inside… it was cooler. Still. Like time had paused just for her.

And there, in the dirt corner where she and her cousin once played marbles, something caught her eye — something shiny, half-buried.

Janna crouched down and dug gently with her fingers. She pulled out a rusted **locket**, thick with dirt but still closed tight. She ran her thumb across the back — faint initials.

M.C.

Her mama's.

Heart thudding, she popped it open.

Inside were two tiny photos. One of her mama — younger than Janna remembered. And next to it… a baby. Wrapped in a floral blanket. Definitely not Janna.

"What the…"

She stared at it, feeling the air drain from her lungs.

Birdie had said to start here. That the truth was in the pasture.

Well, the pasture was speakin'. And what it said?

Was that Maylene Calhoun had a secret baby. And no one ever told Janna Rae a damn thing about it.

Chapter 4 - Darlene's Porch Prophecies

If there was one thing Janna Rae knew for sure, it was this: **Miss Darlene Ferguson knew everything about everybody** — and not always in the order it happened.

She could tell you who was cheatin', who was prayin', and who was both by supper. So if there was a person in Willow's Edge who knew a thing or two about Maylene Calhoun's vanishing act — or the mystery baby in that locket — it was Darlene.

Janna didn't bother calling first. Darlene was the kind of woman who believed folks should "show up proper," not hide behind a phone. Her little white clapboard house sat just past the church, framed by flower pots full of dying petunias and a rusted glider swing that hadn't stopped moving since 1978.

She knocked once. Didn't even have time to shift her weight before the screen door flew open.

"Well I'll be danged," Darlene huffed, hand on hip and apron dusted with flour. "If it ain't Janna Rae Calhoun, risen from the dead and back on my porch."

Janna offered a thin smile. "Afternoon, Miss Darlene."

"I figured you'd come around eventually. I seen Whit Montgomery's car at Birdie's yesterday. Figured it wasn't just a social visit."

"Mind if I sit a spell?"

Darlene stepped aside with a dramatic sweep of her arm. "Honey, that swing's got your name on it. Just try not to break it — the Lord only fixed it twice."

They sat in the heavy silence of early afternoon, cicadas screamin' in the background like overcaffeinated choir singers. Darlene handed her a mason jar of sweet tea without askin'. Janna sipped it once before cuttin' to the chase.

"You remember much about my mama?"

Darlene's eyes didn't move. "Why?"

"I found somethin'. Out by the well house. A locket. Had a picture of her in it… and a baby that ain't me."

Darlene exhaled hard through her nose. "Lord help us."

"So you *do* know somethin'."

"I didn't say that," Darlene snapped, then paused. "But I didn't say I didn't, neither."

Janna turned on the swing to face her full on. "Darlene. I need the truth. Whatever it is. I ain't got time to dance."

Darlene stared into the street like she could see back in time. Her voice dropped.

"Your mama… she had a real hard season right before she left. Started actin' strange. Secretive. She'd disappear for a day or two, come back lookin' worn to the bone. Folks talked, of course. Said she was runnin' off to see a man in the next county, maybe even further. Some thought she was sick. Depressed, even."

Janna gritted her teeth. "Nobody *said* any of this to me."

"We didn't know what was truth and what was smalltown spit. And Birdie? Well, you know how she was.
She kept things close — especially when it came to Maylene."

"So what happened to the baby?"

Darlene's mouth pressed into a tight line.

"That's what nobody knows for sure. Some say she gave it up. Others say… it didn't survive. Birdie never confirmed a thing. Only thing she ever said, and only once, was: *'Maylene didn't leave me nothin' but one child, and I kept her safe.'*"

Janna's heart thumped like a warning bell.

"But maybe," Darlene said slowly, "that wasn't the whole truth."

Chapter 5 - Sawyer's Silence

The feed store hadn't changed much since Janna Rae left town — same crooked OPEN sign, same old bell above the door that dinged about a second too late, and the same smell of sweet grain, tractor grease, and leather.

What had changed… was Sawyer James.

He was behind the counter, sleeves rolled, ball cap backward, loading bags of seed into someone's order slip. His back was broader than she remembered. Or maybe her memory had softened his edges. Either way, her stomach flipped like a fish on dry land.

He didn't see her right away.

Good. She needed a second.

Janna cleared her throat, and that bell finally gave its lazy little *ding*.

Sawyer turned—and froze.

Their eyes locked for just a beat too long.

"Janna Rae."

His voice hadn't changed a lick. Low. Dusty. Like he still swallowed gravel and moonlight.

"Hey, Sawyer," she managed, pretending like her lungs weren't squeezing like a rusty vice. "You got a minute?"

He glanced at the other customer, then handed off the receipt and nodded toward the back.

"Come on. We'll talk out back."

The alley behind the store was shaded, quiet, and scattered with feed sacks and cardboard boxes waitin' to be burned. Sawyer leaned against the wall and crossed his arms like he was bracing himself.

"You're back."

She raised an eyebrow. "Noticed that, did ya?"

"Hard not to. Darlene's been talkin' non-stop since you hit the gravel."

"I'm shocked." She rolled her eyes. "Listen, I didn't come for small talk. I came to ask you a question."

His jaw ticked — a subtle shift, but she caught it.

"Did you know my mama had a baby before she left?"

Sawyer's expression didn't change. But his eyes… oh, his eyes told on him.

"Where'd you hear that?"

"So it's true?"

"I didn't say that."

"But you didn't say it wasn't," she shot back, echoing Darlene's tone.

He exhaled, long and slow. "Look… there were rumors. I was young, but yeah, I remember things goin' quiet real fast around your place. People whisperin'. Then Maylene disappeared, and nobody had the guts to ask questions."

"You didn't think to tell me all this when we were—" She stopped herself. "When we were… younger?"

"I was sixteen, Janna. And by the time I figured out what might've happened… you were already gone."

The silence stretched between them like a frayed rope. Then he added, softer:

"I never forgot you, ya know."

She blinked. "Don't do that."

"Do what?"

"Don't stand there with those sad puppy dog eyes and act like you don't have answers I need. If you know anything else — anything at all — you better start talkin'."

Sawyer hesitated… then reached into his back pocket and pulled out a folded photo.

"I found this about a year ago. It was tucked in the back of the feed office. I didn't know what to make of it then, but now—" He handed it over. "Might mean somethin' to you."

She unfolded it carefully.

It was another picture of her mama. This time she was standing next to a man Janna didn't recognize. Lean, tall, cowboy hat low over his brow. Maylene was holdin' a baby — the same floral blanket. And they were standing right by the fence of **Birdie's pasture.**

There, scrawled in faded ink on the back:

"1977 – M & T – just before goodbye."

Chapter 6 - Truth in the Tall Grass

That night, Janna Rae couldn't sleep. Not with that photo burnin' a hole in her thoughts.

Maylene. The baby. That mystery man with a cowboy hat and a lean build — initials "M & T" scribbled like some half-kept promise. She'd traced those letters with her thumb until her skin went numb. **T.**

Who the hell was "T"?

She needed air. Answers. Maybe a sign from above.

She threw on a flannel shirt, laced her boots, and grabbed the flashlight from the kitchen drawer. The pasture was calling again. She didn't know what she was lookin' for — a clue, a feeling, a memory she hadn't dared to remember — but she *had* to go.

The moon was high, casting soft light over the tall grass as it swayed like it knew secrets too. Janna made her way toward the far fence line, flashlight low, scanning the earth like it might confess.

And then she heard it.

A rustle.

She froze. "Sawyer?"

A shadow stepped forward — tall, broad, familiar.

"It's me," he said quietly, hands in his pockets. "Didn't mean to scare you."

She let out the breath she'd been holdin'. "What are you doin' out here?"

"Could ask you the same."

They stood in silence for a moment, the grass whisperin' around them.

"You said earlier you didn't know who the man in the picture was," she said, "but you hesitated."

Sawyer looked away, jaw clenched. "Because... I recognized the blanket."

"What?"

He turned toward her, eyes dark with something deeper than guilt. "My mama had that same floral baby blanket. I remember it from pictures. She said it belonged to a cousin's baby that didn't make it."

"And you believed that?"

"I was a kid, Janna. I didn't question much." He paused. "But lately... my uncle's been in bad health.

Talkin' in his sleep. Sayin' things about Maylene. About a baby. About *Birdie.*"

Janna's heart sank. "Wait… who's your uncle?"

"**Tucker James.**"
His eyes locked on hers. "Folks around here used to call him **Tuck.**"

Her knees buckled slightly.

"T. As in *M & T*. Maylene and Tuck." She swallowed. "Sawyer… are you sayin'—?"

He looked wrecked. "I think my uncle might be your mama's baby's father. And I think that baby might've been—"
He stopped himself.

"You?" she finished, voice barely a whisper.

"I don't know," he rasped. "I don't know, Janna. But my mama always said Tuck disappeared for a while that summer. That he came back changed. Quiet. Like he'd left something behind."

The silence between them was so loud it hurt.

If that was true… and if the baby had survived… And if Sawyer was *that* baby…

Then that would mean the boy she once loved… was also **her half-brother.**

Chapter 7 - Darlene's Confession

Janna Rae didn't knock this time.

She marched right up Darlene Ferguson's porch, boots thudding like war drums, and flung open the screen door with a creak that could split nerves. The sound of a game show blared from the TV inside, and the smell of biscuits, bacon grease, and denial hung in the air.

Miss Darlene sat at the table, thumbing through a church newsletter and actin' like her porch hadn't just been stormed by a woman on a mission.

"Well, don't you look like a thunderstorm in lipstick," she muttered, folding her paper with dramatic flair. "What's gotten into you now?"

Janna didn't sit. "You knew."

Darlene raised one penciled brow. "You're gonna have to narrow that down, sugar. I know a lotta things."

"You knew my mama had a baby. And you knew **Tuck James** was the father."

Silence fell like a dropped skillet.

Darlene closed her eyes slowly and let out a sigh that sounded twenty years old.

"I was hopin' you wouldn't find that out."

"I did."

Darlene stood and walked to the counter, pouring sweet tea into two mismatched glasses with shaky hands.

She handed one to Janna. "You better sit." Janna

sat.

"I was there," Darlene said finally. "Not in the room, Lord no, but close. Maylene came to me not long before she left town. She was scared, Janna. Real scared. Said Tuck had promised to run off with her, start a life somewhere. But he didn't show."

Janna's grip tightened around the glass.

"She went into labor early. Birdie delivered that baby herself in the back bedroom of that old house. Maylene was a mess — cryin', beggin', sayin' she couldn't do it. That she'd ruined everything. And Birdie…"

She paused, throat tightening.

"Birdie took that baby girl and told Maylene to go. Said she'd handle it. That she'd raise the baby and tell folks it was a cousin's child from upstate. Maylene didn't even fight her. She just... left. Next morning, gone."

Janna blinked. "Wait—baby *girl*?"

Darlene nodded. "That's the part nobody got right. Folks assumed it was a boy 'cause of the James family, but no... that baby was a girl. Named her **Lena** — short for Maylene."

Janna's head spun. "So where is she now?"

"That's the thing." Darlene lowered her voice. "Birdie didn't keep her."

Janna's heart dropped. "What?"

"She sent her away. Told folks she was fostered out to a distant relative in Macon. But I think... I think she was adopted out to someone local. Quietly. Birdie was proud, but she wasn't cruel. She just couldn't raise another baby alone. She did what she thought was best."

"Do you know who has her?"

Darlene hesitated... then nodded.

"I ain't certain... but I believe **Sadie Belle** is her."

Janna nearly choked. "The neighbor girl?! That Sadie?"

"She's sixteen. Real sharp. Came outta nowhere a few years back, got placed with her aunt — that'd be *Lena Ferguson*, my cousin. But Lena couldn't have kids... and suddenly she's got a teenaged 'niece' from 'out of town.' Sounds a little too clean for me."

Janna stood up, the room tilting.

"That girl's been hangin' around my pasture every day..."

"She don't know the truth, Janna. I'm sure of that. But she's yours — in blood."

Janna's knees went weak, and she gripped the back of a chair.

"I have a sister," she whispered. "A half-sister... and she's been standin' right in front of me this whole time."

Darlene nodded, her eyes misty. "And baby, I think Birdie brought you back to help her find her way — the same way she once tried to save your mama."

Chapter 8 - Lena's Bible

Sadie Belle had no business bein' in that house. She knew it, felt it, and ignored it anyway.

Janna wasn't home — off runnin' errands, she figured — so she figured she'd pop over and drop off a basket of fresh peaches like her aunt Lena told her. That part was innocent enough. But then… curiosity done what curiosity always does.

It tugged.

And when Sadie's hand brushed the corner of that old cedar chest in the living room — the one with **Birdie's initials carved in the lid** — well, Lord help her, but she *lifted it.*

Inside were doilies, yellowed recipe cards, a folded apron, and…

A Bible.

Cracked leather, worn spine, and pages edged in gold faded from age.

It wasn't just any Bible. It was **Birdie's** — her name written inside in blue ink, followed by a single sentence in slanted cursive:

"Truth always lives where light ain't yet reached."

Sadie's heart kicked against her ribs.

She opened it.

Tucked inside the front cover was a folded envelope.

She didn't want to open it. She
did open it.

Dear Lena,

I named you after your mama, Maylene. You never
knew her. She never got the chance to know you.

But she loved you. Lord, how she did. She just wasn't
strong enough to stay. And I wasn't strong enough to
keep you.

I made the choice to send you where I thought you'd
be safe. I told your sister — Janna — that she was all
I had. That was a lie I'll carry straight to Heaven.

I reckon the truth will find her one day, just like it
found me. And when it does, I hope she forgives me.
And I hope you do too.

I didn't give birth to you. But I named you. I prayed
over you. I loved you like you were still here.

Don't let the past make you bitter, baby. Let it make you brave. —Birdie

---

Sadie stared at the letter. Eyes wide. Mind spinning.

Lena.
She'd been told her name came from a great-aunt.
That her aunt Lena adopted her from a second cousin in Atlanta after her mama died in a car wreck.

But now? This letter said something different.

And it didn't just change her name. It changed her **everything.**

She stuffed the letter back in the Bible, heart pounding.

Then she heard the screen door creak.

"Sadie?"

Janna Rae's voice echoed into the quiet house.

Sadie's hand froze on the lid of the chest.

She looked down at the letter in the Bible and knew —

Janna Rae Calhoun wasn't just her neighbor.

She was her **sister**.

Chapter 9 - The Pasture Always Knew

The wind was different that morning.

It didn't whip or howl — it whispered. Gentle, steady. Like it had somethin' to say, but only if you were quiet enough to listen.

Janna Rae Calhoun stood in the middle of the pasture, arms crossed, face turned toward the sun that was just startin' to rise over the far tree line. Her boots were damp from dew, her heart heavy as a stone… and yet, there was peace settlin' in her bones. The kind that only comes after the storm's passed and you're still standin'.

She closed her eyes.

Birdie. Maylene. Sawyer. Sadie.
Too many names. Too many questions.
And not a single one with a clean answer.

But somehow, out here, none of that mattered as much.

The grass bowed and swayed around her like it knew her secrets. The soil was soft beneath her heels, the scent of earth and life hangin' thick in the air. She took a slow breath, remembering something Birdie once said:

"You don't have to speak to be heard. Out here, the land listens just fine."

She knelt down, ran her hand through the blades of grass, felt the damp soil between her fingers.

This was where her mama last stood.
Where Birdie made her final choice.
Where the story began — and where it just might end.

The wind carried a quiet memory.

She was nine years old, barefoot and furious, stompin' across this pasture cryin' for her mama. Birdie came after her, slow and steady, never raisin' her voice.

"She's gone, baby. But you're not. So I need you to stay."

Janna didn't understand it then. She did now.

This land didn't just raise her.
It held her grief.
It buried her past.
And now… it was offerin' her a kind of forgiveness she didn't even know she needed.

She stood slowly, brushing her jeans off

The past couldn't be changed.

But the truth? It had finally found its way to the surface — like old roots pushin' up through the dirt.

And Janna was still here. Still breathin'. Still walkin' the pasture.

Not just to remember. But
to start again

Chapter 10 - When the Fence Breaks

Janna Rae didn't sleep that night.

Not after the letter.
Not after Darlene's porch confession.
And sure as sin not after finding Sadie's muddy boot prints by the cedar chest.

She knew the girl had been in the house. And she had a feelin' deep in her gut that Birdie's Bible wasn't in the same spot she left it.

The next morning, Janna found Sadie Belle where she always ended up: perched on the broken fence post at the edge of the pasture, pickin' at the frayed edges of her hoodie like she was unravelin' herself one thread at a time.

Janna walked up slow.

Sadie didn't look at her. Just kicked at a clump of grass with the toe of her worn boot.

"You mad I was in the house?" she asked.

"No," Janna said softly, "I'm mad you didn't tell me sooner."

Sadie looked up, eyes already glassy. "I didn't know what it meant. Not really. That letter… it didn't feel real. I mean, I've always felt different. Like I didn't quite fit. But I never thought—" her voice cracked. "I never thought I'd find out I was a secret."

Janna swallowed hard, kneeling beside her. "You weren't a secret. You were a story nobody was brave enough to tell."

They sat quiet for a while, wind whispering through the tall grass.

Sadie finally asked, "Why didn't Birdie keep me?"

Janna's breath hitched. "Because… she was scared. And she thought she was doin' the right thing. She'd already lost one daughter. She didn't think she could raise another without breakin' in two."

"I just wanted to know her," Sadie whispered.

"She's in you," Janna said, placing her hand on Sadie's. "You've got her eyes. Her fire. And that mouth? Pure Maylene."

That got a laugh. A real one. Small, but true.

"I ain't real good at this sister thing," Janna admitted. "But I'm willin' to learn, if you'll let me."

Sadie blinked, then leaned in — quick and tight —
wrapping her arms around Janna like she'd been
waitin' a lifetime for it.

Janna held on, heart thudding, head full of memories
and futures she never expected.

The fence post creaked beneath them, but held strong.

And maybe that's how they'd be, too.
Bent. Weathered. But
still standin'.

Chapter 11 - Tuck's Truth

The call came just after sundown.

Sawyer's voice on the other end was low, steady, and scratchin' at something deeper than just words.

"He asked for you," he said. "Tuck. Said he wants to talk… before he goes." Janna didn't hesitate.

The James place was dark except for the porch light and a single lamp glowin' through the front window. Inside, the air smelled like old books and lost time. Tuck James lay propped up in a recliner, pale and frail, with a wool blanket draped across his lap and too many years behind his eyes.

He looked up when Janna stepped in.

"You came," he rasped.

"I did."

Sawyer hovered near the doorway, arms folded tight like he was holdin' himself together.

Tuck nodded once. "Good."

Janna eased into the chair across from him, heart thudding. "I need the truth. All of it."

Tuck closed his eyes for a moment. Then opened them again, softer.

"Maylene loved wild. Loved fast. Too much for her own good."
"I didn't mean to hurt her, but I did. I was twenty-two and dumb as fence posts. Told her we'd run off together, start a new life."
"But when I found out she was pregnant... I panicked."
"I left. Didn't even say goodbye. Just... left." Janna

bit the inside of her cheek.

"She waited," he went on. "Waited right here. At Birdie's. Had that baby without me. And I came back months later, full of guilt, thinkin' I'd fix things."

"But Birdie told me to leave. Said I'd done enough damage. Said that baby was hers to protect now. And I... I listened."

He looked down at his hands, as if tryin' to make peace with the dirt still on them.

"I never met her. My daughter. Never got to know her name. And I've carried that ever since." "You mean Sadie," Janna said gently.

Tuck's eyes met hers, misty.

"She alright?"

"She's more than alright," Janna said. "She's brave. Smart. Got more fire in her than a July field."

Tuck let out a breath that sounded like it carried forty years of weight.

"I don't deserve forgiveness."

"No," Janna said. "But she might give it to you anyway."

He nodded, voice shaking. "Tell her I'm sorry. Tell her I was weak."

"I will."

He turned to Sawyer. "And you… thank you for not bein' me."

Sawyer swallowed hard, jaw tight. "You could've been better. But you weren't. That's yours to carry."

Tuck gave a slow nod. "Reckon it is."

An hour later, Janna and Sawyer stood on the porch, the moon hangin' full above them.

"He doesn't have long," Sawyer said quietly.

"No," Janna agreed. "But he gave Sadie somethin' he didn't even know she needed — a name."

They stood in silence a moment longer before Janna added, "And now maybe… we can all move on."

Chapter 12 - Ninety Days

The clock on the wall ticked louder than usual that morning.

Janna Rae sat at the kitchen table with Birdie's Bible open in front of her. Ninety days had come and gone. The pasture outside shimmered in the soft gold light of a Georgia sunrise, peaceful and green — like it knew today mattered.

The land had waited. So had she.

The house felt different now. Lived in. Restored, just enough. Not polished, not perfect — but breathing again.

Like her.

A knock at the screen door pulled her from her thoughts.

Sadie Belle stood there, a paper sack in her hand and a look on her face that said *don't make this harder than it has to be.*

"I brought biscuits," she said, stepping in. "Not from scratch. I ain't Birdie."

Janna smirked. "Well, as long as they don't break teeth, I'll take it."

They sat quietly for a minute, each breaking off a piece of biscuit like they were chewing through time. Sadie finally asked, "So what happens now?"

Janna looked out the window. "Now… I choose."

Sadie swallowed. "You leavin'?"

Janna didn't answer right away.

She thought of her old apartment in the city — the one with walls too white and neighbors she never spoke to.
She thought of the pasture. Of Birdie's voice in the wind. Of Sawyer's silence. Of Tuck's regret. And of the little girl across the fence, who turned out to be her baby sister all along.

"I came back to settle things," Janna said. "But this place unsettled me in ways I didn't expect. I dug up pain I buried deep. Faced people I thought I'd never speak to again. Found out I wasn't the only one carryin' scars."

She looked at Sadie then. Really looked.

"You've got roots here," Janna said softly. "And maybe now… I do too."

Sadie blinked. "You mean…"

"I'm stayin'," Janna said. "If you'll have me."

Sadie didn't speak — she just reached over, wrapped her arms around Janna tight, and held on like she was anchoring herself to the truth.

Later that day, Janna stood at the edge of the pasture, wind brushing her hair back, hands in her pockets.

Sawyer pulled up in his truck, leaned out the window.

"You're still here," he said.

"I am."

He smiled. "Good."

"Don't get too excited," she teased. "I ain't promisin' I'll be nice."

He laughed. "Wouldn't believe it if you did."

They stood in that moment, easy and warm, no rush for the next chapter.

The land had been walked. The truth had been faced.

And for once, the past didn't feel so heavy.

Chapter 13 — Storms Don't Always Bring Rain

The August heat settled low and heavy, like wet cotton stretched across the land. Janna Rae stood at the edge of the pasture, her arms crossed tight against her ribs, watching storm clouds wrinkle the sky but never crack it open. The cows didn't flinch. The wind didn't stir. Everything was just... waiting.

Sawyer had been gone three days. He'd said he was going to Millen to check on some farm equipment, but Janna had a gut feeling he wasn't just chasing parts. He was chasing distance.

She hated that her chest burned every time he left without looking back.

But this time? He'd left his ballcap on the counter and his boots by the door. That said more than words.

Inside the house, Nana Mae was fiddling with an old recipe box, humming a hymn Janna hadn't heard in years. One of those songs where you couldn't tell if it was a prayer or a warning. Janna paused in the doorway, eyes on the woman who raised her without raising her voice.

"There's somethin' you need to know," Nana said, not even turning.

Janna froze. "Is it about Mama?"

"No, baby. It's about your Daddy. And why Sawyer's name ain't just a name on a birth certificate."

Janna's heart pounded so hard she couldn't hear the thunder anymore. There it was — the storm. And it had nothin' to do with weather.

That afternoon spun sideways.

Janna followed Nana Mae to the cedar chest by the back bedroom. A place full of dust, old quilts, and memories that hadn't seen light in years. Tucked between a Bible and a brittle copy of the Millen Weekly from 1986 was a photograph — curled, water-stained, and undeniable.

Her daddy. Young. Smiling. Standing beside a woman who looked too much like Sawyer's mama.

"They were cousins. Close ones. And they were closer than they should've been."

Janna didn't speak for the rest of the evening. She just walked. Past the barn. Through the pasture. Into the quiet places only cows and truth dared to sit.

She wasn't angry. Not yet. She was... unraveling.

Sawyer wasn't just her past.

He might be tied to her in ways that would tangle the whole story she thought she was living.

Back at the house, Nana Mae watched from the porch swing. A single tear slid down her cheek, not from sorrow — but from the knowing.

Storms don't always bring rain.
Sometimes, they bring answers.

Chapter 14 – The Long Way Home

Janna Rae didn't sleep much that night. The floor creaked under restless steps as she paced the house barefoot, trying to find where the truth ended and her life began. The photo was still in her back pocket, bent from being clutched too tight.

By sunrise, she'd already fed the chickens, tossed hay to the cattle, and boiled coffee strong enough to wake the dead.

"I'm takin' a ride," she called out to Nana Mae, grabbing her keys.

"To where?" Nana asked from the porch.

"Wherever this mess started."

Waynesboro was the first stop. It was where Daddy used to meet with folks from the co-op, where Sawyer's mama once worked the register at Turner's Hardware. Janna drove slow through town, eyes scanning for anything that looked the same. It all did. That was the problem.

Outside the hardware store, Mr. Clint — long retired but never far from gossip — stood with a coffee in hand. He nodded as she walked up.

"Ain't seen your face around here in a spell."

"Looking for a memory," Janna replied, "or maybe the truth."

"Same thing, most days," he said. "You check Statesboro yet?"

By mid-morning, she was halfway to **Statesboro**, windows down, wind tangling her hair like it used to when Sawyer would drive and she'd just listen to the engine hum between them.

There was a woman there, Miss Ellamae, who used to babysit Janna when her daddy had business in Augusta. She still lived off North College Street, surrounded by cats, potted plants, and more wisdom than the Internet ever dreamed of.

"Your daddy?" Ellamae said, stirring sweet tea so thick it barely moved. "He was a good man. But he was caught in a knot tied long before you or Sawyer were born."

"So it's true?" Janna asked.

"Baby girl," she sighed, "sometimes family trees got crooked limbs. But that don't mean the roots are bad."

That night, Janna stopped in **Savannah**, just long enough to sit near the river and breathe in salt and silence. She thought about running. About never going back. Savannah always had that effect — tempting and beautiful, like trouble in high heels.

But something pulled her back. Not obligation. Not guilt. **Home.**

Two days later, she drove straight to **Augusta**, walked into a records office, and requested everything she could legally get. Births. Deaths. Marriage licenses. Adoption filings. Her fingers shook as she sifted through faded forms and courthouse seals.

There it was.
A name.
One that changed everything.

"Nana Mae," she whispered to herself, "you've been protectin' more than just me."

By the time she pulled back into Millen, the sun was falling low and orange, the cows were grazing quiet, and Nana Mae was sitting exactly where she always did — on the porch, with a glass of peach tea and a look that said *she already knew.*

"You took the long way 'round," she said.

"Had to," Janna replied. "I needed to know who I was."

"And did you?"

Janna sat beside her, took the tea, and watched the pasture breathe.

"I think I'm just gettin' started."

Chapter 15 – The Silence Between Answers

Janna didn't speak for a full day after coming back from Augusta. She swept the porch. Fed the hens. Stirred Nana Mae's stew without saying a word. Not because she didn't have something to say, but because she didn't know where to start.

There was no easy way to ask your grandmother why your father's name was on **someone else's birth record**.

Or why the woman Sawyer always believed was his mother… wasn't.

That evening, the pasture was quiet as a hymn. Not the kind you sing in church — the kind that lives in your bones. She wandered down by the tree line, the place where she used to sit as a girl and pretend her worries could be buried under ant beds and cow pies.

Sawyer's truck pulled in around dusk. She could hear it before she saw it — that same knocking sound in the exhaust, like a heartbeat gone sideways.

He didn't get out at first.

When he did, he didn't walk toward her. Just leaned on the tailgate like a man bracing himself for news he already knew.

"You went diggin'," he said finally.

"I needed to know what I was built from."

"And did you?"

"Some of it," she replied. "But the rest, I think you've got in your pocket."

Sawyer looked down, jaw tight. "I've always felt like I didn't fit," he muttered. "Mama — well, the one who raised me — she loved me, sure. But she kept distance like it was part of the chore list."

Janna took a few slow steps toward him. "You were born here. But you weren't raised in truth." "And you think I should hate her for that?"

"No," she said. "I think you should sit with it."

"And you? What are you gonna do?"

Janna swallowed hard. "I'm gonna figure out how to move forward without letting the past poison everything I still believe in."

They didn't hug. They didn't cry. They just stood there — two people shaped by the same broken roots, tryin' to learn how to grow anyway.

Back at the house, Nana Mae sat at the kitchen table, an old shoebox in front of her. Inside were letters. Dozens. Yellowed, handwritten, and sealed with the kind of love that lives on borrowed time.

"I was gonna burn 'em," she said softly as Janna walked in.

"Why didn't you?"

"Because I knew someday you'd ask the kind of questions only ashes can't answer."

Janna picked up the first envelope, her hands shaking.

It was addressed to her daddy.
From Sawyer's mother.
The one who wasn't supposed to know how to love.
But who, in every line of ink, proved she absolutely did.

"The truth," Nana Mae whispered, "don't always set you free. But it will sure as heaven set you straight."

Outside, thunder rumbled low — not the kind that brings storms.
The kind that clears the sky.

Chapter 16 – Not All Roots Run Deep

The next morning came without much color. Gray light spilled through the curtains like it was apologizing for waking her. Janna Rae sat at the kitchen table, still in her nightgown, clutching the last letter from the box.

It wasn't from Sawyer's mother this time.

It was from her own.

A name she hadn't spoken in years — **Marla Calhoun** — written in handwriting that trembled between anger and apology.

"If you're reading this, Janna, then I know you've found out. About your daddy. About the boy. About everything I tried to keep you from. I never meant to leave you with more questions than memories…"

She read every line twice. Some parts made her chest hurt. Others made her furious. Her mama had left when Janna was only nine, blaming farm life for her dried-up dreams and a man who loved the land more than he loved her.

But this letter… it told a different story.

It told of betrayal. Of family pressure. Of Nana Mae choosing to send Marla away when things got too complicated — too scandalous.

And it told of **a half-sibling**, born in **Savannah**, who had been quietly adopted out before Janna was even old enough to remember her mama leaving.

Her spoon clattered in the sink as her knees weakened.

"There's more," she whispered to herself. "There's *another one of us* out there."

She looked out the window, past the fence line, past the barn, past everything she'd ever known.

And for the first time, she realized:
Millen wasn't the whole story. It was just the beginning.

Later that evening, Sawyer found her back down at the tree line again — her boots half sunk in mud, the letter tucked in her pocket.

"You okay?" he asked.

"Not yet," she said. "But I will be. I have to be.

There's somebody out there I'm supposed to find."
"You think she wants to be found?"

"I don't know. But I think I need her more than she needs me."

Sawyer didn't ask more. Just reached down, plucked a stick from the ground, and started drawin' circles in the dirt beside her.

"You're like this place, Janna," he said after a while. "A little worn, a little stubborn... but you sure as hell hold your ground."

She smiled, even though her throat ached.

"And you?" she asked.

"I'm like that broken gate on the east side of the fence," he said. "Still hangin' on. But Lord, do I creak."

They both laughed — not because it was funny, but because it was human.

Back at the house, the shoebox was empty now.

But Janna's heart was just starting to fill.

Chapter 17 – The Girl in Savannah

The next morning, Janna Rae stood in front of the mirror, brush in one hand, mama's letter in the other. Her hair was a tangled mess, much like her thoughts — but she tugged through it anyway. She had miles to go, and no room left for hesitation.

"Savannah," she said aloud, like tasting the word for the first time.
"Let's see what you've been hiding."

By mid-morning, the old Silverado was aimed southeast, tires humming steady down Highway 25. She passed **Statesboro**, waved silently at the exits she now knew by heart, and kept going until the air got thicker and the moss hung lower.

The streets of **Savannah** rolled out like an old quilt — cobblestone, cracked sidewalks, and houses that had seen too much and said too little. It smelled like river salt and forgotten promises.

She didn't have much to go on — just the first name in the letter: **"Laurel."** Born 1985.

Placed with a private adoption agency by Marla Calhoun.
No last name. No address. No clue if she was still alive or living three doors down.

But Janna didn't need a full map. Just a starting point.

She began with **St. Mark's Family Agency**, one of the oldest in Chatham County. The receptionist, a young woman with tightly wound curls and halflenses on her nose, looked up when Janna approached.

"Can I help you?"

"Maybe," Janna said. "I'm looking for a woman. Her name is Laurel. I think she was adopted through here."

"We don't release adoption records."

"I figured you'd say that." Janna pulled the letter from her bag. "But this ain't about paperwork. It's about blood."

The woman looked at her for a long second, then softened slightly.

"You'd be surprised how many folks come in here with pieces of a puzzle they didn't ask for," she said. "And even more surprised how often those pieces line up."

By the time Janna left, she didn't have an address — but she had something better.

A hint.

"Try the artisan shop off River Street," the receptionist said. "Girl named Laurel runs it. She's about your age. Looks a bit like you, if I'm honest."

River Street shimmered in the early afternoon haze. Tourists wandered past cafés and ironwork balconies. But Janna only saw one thing: a little brick storefront with a white shiplap sign that read:
"Laurel & Sage — Handmade Southern Wares."

The bell over the door jingled as she stepped inside. Dried lavender hung from the beams, and the place smelled like beeswax and old magnolia. It was soft, curated… warm.

And behind the counter stood a woman with auburn hair pulled into a braid and eyes the exact same shade as Janna's.

"Hi there," the woman said. "Welcome to Laurel & Sage."

Janna couldn't speak. Her voice caught in her throat like a fishhook.

The woman tilted her head. "Are you okay?"

"I… think I might be your sister."

The world paused.

The fans stopped spinning. The clock stopped ticking. Even Janna's heart seemed to skip a beat.

Laurel didn't gasp. Didn't faint. She just stared — and then, with a calm that felt like déjà vu, stepped around the counter.

"Let's talk," she said, leading Janna to a little back room with a velvet loveseat and an old coffee table.

"And maybe… let's not tell each other everything at once."

Chapter 18 – Salt in the Blood

Janna Rae never imagined her life would take her
from cow fields and pine trees to lavender candles
and vintage chandeliers — but here she was, in the
back room of a boutique on River Street, trying not to
cry in front of a woman who shared her eyes.

Laurel sat cross-legged on the loveseat, one hand
wrapped around a mug of chamomile tea, the other
holding the letter Janna had brought.

"I don't know what I'm supposed to feel," Laurel
finally whispered.
"Relieved? Angry? Like I missed out? Or like I was
spared?"

"I don't know either," Janna said. "But I figure we
don't have to figure it all out today."

They spent the next few hours talking. Nothing heavy.
Just the kinds of things sisters might talk about if
they'd grown up side-by-side.

"You ever been to Tybee?" Laurel asked suddenly.

"Couple times. Daddy used to take me and my
cousins for beach days. We'd pack bologna
sandwiches, Fritos, and a red-and-white Igloo cooler.

Daddy'd never swim, but he'd sit under an umbrella like a king."

Laurel laughed, her voice soft like ocean foam.

"My folks had a condo there. Tybee was my second home. I learned how to surf... sort of."

"We used driftwood for swords," Janna smirked. "You probably had sunscreen. We had sunburns and watermelon slices straight off the tailgate."

"We both had salt in the blood, though."

They smiled at that. Because somehow, it felt true.

Later that week, Laurel closed the shop for two days and invited Janna on a sister's getaway.

"Let's go to **Jekyll Island**," she said. "I've got a friend with a cottage. We can talk or not talk. Walk the beach. Clear our heads."

And they did.

They sat by the dunes under a sky full of stars, barefoot, holding mugs of coffee at midnight while the tide whispered things too sacred for daylight. They spoke about the past — the good, the ugly, the unanswered.

"Did you ever hate her?" Laurel asked.

"Mama?" Janna blinked. "Sometimes. But mostly I just missed her, even when I didn't remember why."

Jekyll healed something soft between them — not completely, but just enough to build a bridge.

And when the weekend ended, they hugged like they'd always known how.

Back in Millen, Nana Mae watched from the porch as Janna pulled into the drive, red dust trailing behind her.

"You look different," she said, handing Janna a glass of sweet tea.

"I feel different."

"That girl your sister?"

"She is now."

Janna didn't say much more. Just kicked off her boots, curled up in her daddy's old recliner, and thought about what it meant to be a woman built on land and loss... but still able to laugh with someone who'd lived a whole other life.

She thought about **Panama City Beach**, where her mama once promised they'd go — and never did.

She thought about **St. Augustine**, where Laurel's adoptive mama taught her how to play the piano in a little yellow cottage.

And she thought about *forgiveness.*

Not the easy kind.
The kind that takes years to speak out loud. The kind that starts as a whisper inside your own bones.

Chapter 19 – The Weight of Quiet Places

It rained the next morning — just enough to leave little puddles in the grooves of the dirt road and fog the windows of the kitchen. Janna stood barefoot by the screen door, coffee in hand, watching the drops slide off the eaves like old memories.

"Storm's past," Nana Mae said behind her. "But the air's still heavy."

"Yeah. So's my heart."

After breakfast, Janna grabbed the rusted ring of keys from the nail by the back door — the same ring her daddy used to carry in his overalls. She walked through the side yard, the red mud sticking to her boots, and made her way to the barn.

The hinges creaked just like they used to. The smell inside hit her square in the chest: hay, motor oil, dust, and time.

She stepped across the threshold like entering a church.

"I used to hide in here when Mama'd cry," she whispered to the silence. "Sometimes I'd talk to the horse stalls like they could answer."

The loft above still held the old hay bales, but now, light came through in slats, slicing the air into golden bars. She climbed the ladder, her palm brushing the rails that once scraped her knuckles when she was ten and angry at the world.

There, in the far corner, beneath a stained horse blanket, was the box.

Not *the* shoebox — that was tucked safe in her suitcase now — but another. Bigger. Older. Untouched since the day her daddy passed.

She opened it slowly.

Inside were:

- Two old Polaroids of her and Sawyer as kids
- A pocketknife with her initials carved in the handle
- A crumpled napkin with "*Laurel — 1985*" scribbled in her mama's handwriting
- And a small envelope marked: **"For When She Comes Home."**

Janna's breath hitched.

"Did you know, Daddy?" she whispered. "Did you know all along?"

She unfolded the note.

"Janna — I reckon if you're readin' this, you've walked through more than I ever could've prepared you for. I didn't have all the answers, and I sure didn't always do things right. But I prayed you'd be strong enough to find what I never could say."

"There's things the barn knows. Things I left behind out here 'cause I didn't know how to bring them into the house."

"If you've found Laurel... love her like you always would've. She's got your heart. And she's gonna need it."

"Love, Daddy."

Janna sat there for a long while, the old boards beneath her groaning like they remembered too.

The barn had waited.
It had kept the quiet.
But it had never truly been silent.

Not to her.

By the time the sun peeked out and dried the puddles, she climbed back down and closed the doors behind her.

"Alright, old girl," she said to the barn. "You held your end. Now it's my turn."

Chapter 20 – Two Chairs and One Truth

The porch swing creaked a little louder than usual that evening, like it, too, had something to say.

Janna sat on one end, her knees tucked up close, and Laurel sat on the other, barefoot and quiet, watching the fireflies blink in the front yard. Between them sat a pitcher of sweet tea, two glasses already sweating in the Georgia heat.

The kind of night where the air hangs heavy with things folks haven't said.

"I went into the barn today," Janna finally said.

"You always talked about it like it was a person," Laurel replied, half-smiling.

"Sometimes I think it was."

She handed Laurel the note. Watched her read it slow. Watched her shoulders shift — just enough to let something in.

"He knew," Laurel whispered.

"Yeah. He did."

They sat there for a long time, both of them holding pieces of the same broken plate, slowly figuring out how to glue it back together.

"You ever think," Laurel asked, "that maybe we were meant to find each other now — not then?"

"Maybe. Maybe if we'd met as kids, we would've torn each other apart."

Laurel laughed softly.

"Two stubborn girls fighting over who got more cornbread."

"Or who could climb higher in the barn loft."
"You'd have lost." "Excuse
you?"

They both burst out laughing, the kind of laugh that feels like medicine and memory all at once.

When the night got quiet again, Janna poured the last of the tea and leaned back.

"There's a lot I still don't know," she said. "About Mama. About what happened."

"Same here."

"But I think the truth's not always in the answers. Sometimes it's in the *askin'*."

"Or in the listenin'."

Later, after Laurel went to bed, Janna stayed out on the swing.

The stars were out now — clear and bright — like pinholes poked in the curtain of heaven. The barn stood off in the distance, barely lit by the porch glow.

Janna whispered into the night:

"I'm gonna do right by this.
Not just for me. Not just for Laurel.
But for the barn.
For what it knows.
For what it kept safe 'til I was ready."

Inside the house, an old clock ticked soft on the mantel.
But outside?

That porch held two empty chairs and one truth...

And they were finally ready to fill 'em.

Chapter 21 – Dust Don't Settle Easy in Millen

The next morning started the way most did in Millen — with the sound of a screen door slappin' shut and the faint hum of gossip brewing across back fences.

At Nana Mae's kitchen table, the coffee was hot, the bacon was louder than the news, and Janna was deep in thought.

"You got that look in your eye," Nana Mae said, stirring her grits.
"What look?"
"The 'I'm fixin' to stir something up' look. Same one your mama used to get."

Janna cracked a grin but didn't deny it.

"I think it's time I start tellin' folks Laurel's here."

That afternoon, she pulled her truck into town, Laurel in the passenger seat — eyes wide, lips tight, heart pounding under a borrowed ball cap.

"You sure 'bout this?" Laurel asked. "No.
But I'm doin' it anyway."

The old feed store still had a Coca-Cola bench out front, and three men who hadn't moved since 1982 sat on it like prophets watchin' the world unfold. Janna stepped out of the truck and nodded.

"Afternoon, boys."
"Well I'll be," one of 'em said. "Janna Rae Calhoun. Thought you left us for good."
"I tried. But the dirt here's got claws." "That it does."

She motioned to Laurel.

"This here's my sister. Laurel."

Three mouths fell open in slow motion. One spit his chew and missed the can.

"Well... I'll be double-dog-darned."

By the time they hit the diner for pie, the town had already started whisperin'.

"They'll talk," Laurel said.
"They always do," Janna replied. "Let 'em get it out of their system."

At the church that Sunday, some folks stared. A few hugged. One older woman leaned over and said:

"I always thought your mama looked tired back then. Now I know why."

By midweek, the whispers had faded into nods. And one afternoon, Pastor Royce stopped by the farm.

He didn't say much — just sat on the porch, hat in hand.

"Sometimes God don't give answers, Janna," he said. "He gives people."

"I'll take that."

That night, the barn creaked in the breeze — not like it was complainin', but like it approved.

The weight of secrets was heavy. But now, shared?

It was finally shiftin'.

Chapter 22 – Something Worth Planting

Janna stood in the garden behind the barn, boots sunk in soft dirt, hands on her hips. The tomato vines had gone wild since spring — growing tall and tangled like the family story she'd just untwisted.

Laurel walked out barefoot, holding two mugs of sweet tea.

"You always work when you're thinking?"

"Only when thinking gets too loud."

They sipped in silence for a while, watching a red bird flit from fencepost to tree.

"You ever wonder," Laurel asked, "why Daddy never just… told the truth?"

Janna didn't answer right away. She knelt down and yanked a stubborn weed from the soil.

"Some folks were raised to bury their feelings deeper than fence posts. Doesn't mean they didn't love us."

"Just means they didn't know how to say it?"

"Exactly."

That afternoon, Janna drove out to Statesboro.
Not for errands. Not to run.
She had an idea. A calling, even.

She stopped by an old building just off the highway
— a wide tin-roofed thing with peeling paint and
stories in its bones. Once a general store. Then a feed
mill. Now? Nothing but dust and leftover ghosts.

She walked around the back, taking notes in her head.

A week later, Laurel helped her scrub the floors.
Nana Mae brought sandwiches.
Sawyer donated lumber.
And Pastor Royce showed up with paint.

They were rebuilding something.

"What is this place gonna be?" Laurel asked one day,
wiping sweat from her brow.

"A space," Janna replied. "For girls like us.
Girls who never got answers.
Girls who carried silence like it was their name."

By fall, the sign was hung:

"The Porchlight Project" *Come
sit. Come heal. Come home.*

In Millen, they still talked — but now, they talked
with Janna instead of **about** her.

And when she got up early to check the garden, or
opened the barn just to let in the light, she did it with
a kind of peace that didn't used to live inside her.

She'd found something worth planting. And
this time, it wasn't just tomatoes.

Chapter 23 – The Porchlight Stays On

The ribbon-cutting ceremony wasn't flashy. There weren't balloons or a fancy mayor's speech, just a long picnic table covered in a gingham cloth, a crockpot full of Nana Mae's pulled pork, and folks gathered under the creak of that old tin roof.

The Porchlight Project was officially open.

It started as an idea — but now?
It was a place. A safe one.
Where questions didn't need permission, and answers didn't need perfection.

Janna stood by the front door, hands dusted with sawdust, hair pulled back, wearing her mama's old pearl-button shirt like armor.

"You nervous?" Laurel asked beside her.

"More like… proud."

"You should be. You didn't just build this place. You *rebuilt us*."

Janna looked around at the crowd: teenagers, young mamas, quiet older women with eyes that had seen too much. Sawyer leaning on the porch railing. Nana Mae with her hand on her heart.

"I didn't fix everything," she whispered.
"No. But you gave it somewhere to heal."

After the blessing, folks took turns writing on the chalkboard inside — one word that described what they needed:

Hope. Grace. Peace. Forgiveness. A chance.

And by sundown, the porchlight was glowing warm against the night.

That week, a letter came in the mail — postmarked from Savannah.

It was from her mama.

The handwriting looked older. Worn. Like it hadn't been used in a long while.

Janna stared at it for a full five minutes before opening it.

Janna,

I know this letter's late — maybe too late. But I heard about the barn. About Laurel. About you.
I don't have excuses. Just silence. And I'm ready to stop carrying that now.
If you'll have me, I'd like to come home. Not to stay. Just to sit on the porch awhile. Maybe talk. Maybe not.
But I miss you.
And I never stopped loving you. Even when I didn't know how to show it.

Mama

Janna didn't cry. Not right then.
She folded the letter slow, ran her fingers across the crease like it was the ridge of a long-forgotten mountain, and set it on the table.

Then she walked out to the porch, turned the switch, and watched the glow spill out again.

"The porchlight stays on," she whispered. "Always has. Always will."

Chapter 24 – She Came in Quiet

It was a Tuesday.
Not a Sunday. Not a holiday.
Just a regular, no-fuss Tuesday when the wind carried the scent of honeysuckle through the pines.

Janna was watering the porch plants when she saw the silver sedan turn up the drive.

She knew that car.
Hadn't seen it in over fifteen years — but the way it eased down the road, like it was tiptoeing across sacred ground… there was no mistaking it.

Laurel stepped out onto the porch, hands tucked in the sleeves of her flannel.

"Is that her?"

Janna nodded.

The car door opened slow. A figure stepped out — thinner than Janna remembered, a little stooped, hair streaked with silver, but her eyes… Lord, those eyes still held the weight of two decades gone.

It was her mama.

They didn't rush.
Didn't cry.
Didn't yell or hug or say all the things they once
rehearsed in their own minds.

Janna simply opened the screen door and said:

"There's coffee in the kitchen. And a chair with your
name on it."

Her mama stepped onto the porch like a woman
walking on holy ground.

They sat. Three women.
One table.
And more truth between them than any words could
ever carry.

It took a while for anyone to speak. The mug in her
mama's hand trembled slightly as she lifted it.

"I thought I'd forgotten the way this house smelled,"
she said.
"But I didn't. Not one bit."

"You never wrote back," Janna said softly.
"I didn't know what to say."
"The truth would've done fine."

Laurel watched them, quiet as a shadow, then finally asked:

"Why'd you leave?"

Her mama looked down at her cup. Then at the barn. Then back at them.

"Because I didn't believe I belonged here. And because I was afraid… I'd ruin you if I stayed."

There it was. No excuses. Just fear, raw and cracked open.

"You didn't ruin us," Janna said.
"You just made us figure out how to grow with holes."

Silence again. But it wasn't cold this time.

It was the kind of silence that made room for healing.

As the sun lowered behind the barn, they sat longer.

"I don't expect forgiveness," her mama said. "But I'm askin' for a little grace."

"Well," Janna said, "You're in Georgia. We hand it out by the pitcher."

And just like that, the past took off its boots and came inside.

Not perfect.
Not whole.
But finally… home.

Chapter 25 – The Things We Keep

A few days after her mama's visit, Janna found herself in the attic.

She hadn't been up there in years — not since the summer after high school when she'd boxed up old yearbooks and trophies and promised herself she was *done with this town.*

The air smelled like cedar and dust.
Cobwebs danced in the sunlight pouring through the one square window.
She carried a lantern, just in case the bulb flickered out — but mostly, she carried a sense that she wasn't alone.

In the far corner, covered by an old quilt with sunflowers stitched in the corners, sat a trunk.

Her daddy's.
With the initials **WRC** carved in the brass clasp — *William Ray Calhoun.*

She hesitated.
Then knelt down and opened it.

Inside were layers of time:

- A Sunday tie with a faded grease stain
- A Cracker Jack prize still in the wrapper
- A Polaroid of Janna on a tricycle, Sawyer holding a fishing pole beside her
- And tucked inside a folded bandana… a letter

The envelope read:
"To my girls. When the time's right."

Janna sat down on a stack of old books and opened it slow.

"If you're reading this, then the dust has settled some. Maybe not all the way. But enough for you to see clear."

"I didn't always speak easy, but I saw everything. I saw how strong you were, Janna, even when you were breakin'. I saw Laurel in the swing set's shadow when you thought no one noticed. And I knew one day… you'd find your way back to each other."

"There's love that speaks, and love that holds its tongue. I was the second kind. Doesn't mean it ran shallow."

"Let the past have its place, but don't live there. The porchlight ain't for ghosts — it's for the living. Keep it on. Keep it warm. And keep each other."

"Love you forever, Daddy."

She read it twice. Then a third time.
And by the time she folded it and tucked it close to her chest, her tears had already soaked through the top of her shirt.

She wasn't crying from pain this time.

She was crying from peace.

Later that night, Janna brought the letter down and placed it inside a cedar frame on the mantel.

"This house," she whispered, "wasn't built on brick. It was built on forgiveness."

And upstairs, in that attic full of memories, the air felt lighter than it had in years.

Chapter 26 – The Sound of Roots Growing

The fall wind had shifted — not in force, but in feeling.
There was something *new* in the air. Not the kind that carried storms, but the kind that whispered, *"Stay a while."*

Janna stood at the edge of the pasture, boots planted in worn grass, arms folded as she watched the herd move slow in the golden light.

The barn stood behind her, strong and still — but the real growth? It was happening inside of her now.

Laurel had taken to helping in the mornings — feeding chickens, gathering eggs, sweeping the porch before the dew could settle in.

She no longer asked, "How long am I staying?"

Now, she just said:

"You want the hens or the hayloft?"

Sawyer showed up every Thursday with new lumber scraps "just in case," though Janna had a sneakin' suspicion he didn't care about wood so much as the *company*.

He never pressed. Never pried. Just showed up — the way good men do.

"Still got that hammer swing?" he asked one morning, handing her a nail pouch.

"Still better than yours," she grinned.

Nana Mae started hosting story circles at The Porchlight Project every Saturday. Folks came from *Waynesboro, Statesboro, even Savannah* just to sit, sip sweet tea, and tell pieces of themselves they'd never said aloud.

And Janna?
She finally bought herself a new journal.

On the first page, she wrote:

"Some things break. Some things bloom. And sometimes... you get both, all in the same season."

One afternoon, Janna and Laurel drove down to **Panama City Beach**, just to breathe somewhere different.
They sat in the sand, toes dug deep, hair tangled by salt and wind.

"You ever think we'd end up like this?" Laurel asked.

"Not even in my wildest dreams," Janna said.
"But I'm glad we did."

As the sun melted into the water, Laurel leaned over and said:

"I think Daddy would be proud of you."

Janna smiled, tears slipping without shame.

"I think... I'm finally proud of me, too."

Chapter 27 – The Calhoun Name Still Holds

The first frost rolled in with a whisper — not loud, not rude, just a gentle reminder that seasons don't wait on anybody.

Janna pulled her jacket tight as she walked the fence line.
The calves had come in close to the barn. The wind carried a bite, but she welcomed it.

There was a quiet peace in the work now — not the kind that came from escaping, but the kind you find when you've come full circle.

Back at the house, a letter had arrived from a high school student in **Augusta**.

It was handwritten on notebook paper with a header that read:

"I heard about The Porchlight Project… and I think you might understand me."

The girl's name was *Lila*.

Seventeen.
Pregnant.
And scared as all get out.

"I don't want advice. I just want to know if I'm broken."

Janna read it twice. Then again.

Then she sat down at the old kitchen table and wrote back:

"Dear Lila,
No, baby — you ain't broken. You're just cracked open enough for the light to get in."

"Come see us when you're ready. We'll leave the porchlight on."

That same week, Sawyer asked if she'd be willing to speak at the **Millen County Harvest Festival** — a first-ever panel about local women making a difference.

She nearly laughed out loud.

"Me? I ain't no speaker."
"You're more than a speaker," he said.
"You're a story still being written — and people need to hear you read it out loud."

So she did.

Nervous as a long-tailed cat in a room full of rockers, she stood on that creaky festival stage in front of old classmates, former Sunday school teachers, kids selling boiled peanuts, and a whole town that used to whisper her name.

"I'm Janna Rae Calhoun," she said into the mic, her voice steady.
"And I used to think this place was too small for me. Turns out, it's exactly the size of my healing."

The crowd clapped. A few cried.
One old fella even stood and said, *"The Calhoun name still holds in this town. Stronger than ever."*

That night, Laurel hugged her tight before bed.

"You know what I think?" she asked. "What's that?"

"I think the barn knew all along. It just waited for you to be ready."

Janna looked out the window one last time before turning off the lamp.

The barn stood tall under the stars, just as it always had.

Silent.
Solid.
Sacred.

Chapter 28 – Where the Wind Don't Lie

The morning after the festival, Janna sat on the back porch with a blanket wrapped around her shoulders and her coffee mug resting on her knees.

The world was quiet — not because it was empty, but because it was *settled.*

She could hear cows lowin' out in the pasture. The barn creaked softly in the breeze. And for the first time in what felt like forever, her *mind* matched the pace of the land.

But quiet don't always mean easy.

The phone rang mid-morning.
It was the hospital in **Savannah**.
Her mama had collapsed at her job — low blood sugar, exhaustion, stress. They said she'd be okay, but she needed rest… and someone to take her home.

Janna didn't hesitate.

She packed a bag, kissed Nana Mae on the cheek, left Laurel in charge of the hens, and hit the road.

The drive was long — not in miles, but in memories.

She passed **Statesboro**, where she and Sawyer once slow-danced behind a bonfire.
Then **Waynesboro**, where her mama used to take them school shopping before things fell apart. Then finally, Savannah — wide and bustling, so unlike Millen… and yet still full of pieces of her.

When she walked into the hospital room, her mama looked up with tired eyes.

"You didn't have to come," she whispered.

"Yes, I did."

"I was doin' better. I promise I was tryin'."

Janna sat down at the edge of the bed and reached for her hand.

"I know. But you don't have to prove anything. Not to me. Not anymore."

They rode home in silence, windows cracked, the wind blowin' just enough to carry their thoughts.

"This air," her mama finally said, "it smells like forgiveness."

"That's 'cause the wind don't lie around here," Janna replied. "It just tells the truth real slow."

Back home, Laurel had made stew. Sawyer brought over firewood.

And Janna tucked her mama into the old guest room — the same one that once held pain and now held peace.

That night, before bed, she wrote one line in her journal:

"I'm not tryin' to fix the past anymore. I'm just learning how to live beside it."

Chapter 29 – Things With Wings

The barn was full that Saturday.

Not with hay, or horses, or tools — but with voices.

Lila from Augusta had come, belly round and eyes wide.
Miss Edie from Waynesboro brought cornbread muffins in a floral tin.
Two sisters from Tybee Island carried beach wind in their hair and nervous laughter in their hearts.

They all came for the same thing: a place where silence didn't win.

Janna stood near the side door, arms crossed loosely, watchin' the women settle onto quilt-covered hay bales.

Laurel gave the welcome.

"We ain't here to fix each other.
We're here to be *with* each other."

The stories came easy.

One girl talked about losing her brother.

Another about growing up too fast.

Miss Edie confessed she hadn't danced in twenty years because her husband once told her she "looked silly."

Janna took a deep breath and shared her own truth.

"I once believed that healing came after forgiveness. Turns out, sometimes healing comes first… and makes forgiveness possible."

That night, after everyone left, Janna stayed back in the barn.

The moonlight poured in through the cracks in the walls like silver lace.

And in the rafters above, a single dove had built a nest — nestled right where the beams met in the shape of a cross.

She stared up at it, smiling.

"Well, would ya look at that," she whispered. "Even this barn holds things with wings."

The next morning, she found a small feather on the barn floor.

She tucked it into her journal, right between the pages where she'd written her father's letter and her mama's return.

Not all legacies are made of land and money.

Some are made of feathers, barn dust, and the courage to speak your name out loud.

Chapter 30 – The Fall Jubilee

If there was one thing Millen knew how to do right, it was a Fall Jubilee.

Every year, come October, the downtown square lit up with hayrides, kettle corn, and homemade jams stacked in rows like trophies of Southern pride.

But this year?

This year, they asked **Janna Rae Calhoun** to be the **Grand Marshal**.

She laughed when she got the call.

"Me? Lead the parade? I ain't no baton twirler."

"You're more than that," the mayor's secretary replied.
"You're the reason half the town's found their way home again."

So on the second Saturday in October, Janna climbed up onto the front bench of a wagon pulled by two chestnut horses, Laurel at her side, and Sawyer walkin' ahead leadin' the reins.

Nana Mae sat behind them, tossin' peppermints to the crowd like a queen on her coronation day.

The banner read:

"Honoring the Calhoun Legacy – Faith, Family, and the Porchlight Project."

Kids waved. Old timers nodded with pride. The smell of fried pies floated through the air.

Janna wore boots scuffed with purpose and a denim jacket with a little heart stitched on the sleeve — made by Laurel.

And when they passed the barn on the edge of town, Sawyer tipped his hat.

"That ol' girl's never looked prouder," he said. "Neither have you."

Later that night, under the string lights hung across the square, a slow song played from a dusty speaker.

Sawyer held out his hand.

"Wanna dance, Janna Rae?"

"Here? In front of everybody?"

"Why not?"

"Well… alright then."

They moved slow. Comfortable. Familiar. Like two folks who didn't need a crowd to feel seen.

"You think we made it?" she asked.
"Made what?"
"A life worth stayin' for."

Sawyer smiled, pulling her just a little closer.

"I think we're still makin' it. One fencepost at a time."

And overhead, the stars blinked like they were proud of her, too.

Chapter 31 –
What Comes Back

The days grew shorter, but the light inside the house stayed long.

Janna Rae stood at the kitchen window, stirring a pot of stew, while her mama shelled peas at the table. Laurel folded linens. Sawyer patched the fence line out back.

Nobody said it, but *everybody knew*:
They'd become a family again — not because of blood, but because of **choice.**

Chapter 32 –
Letters to the Future

She started writing letters — to women she hadn't met yet.
Each one sealed and tucked into a wooden box at the barn entrance.

"Dear You," one read,
"You're gonna make it. Not because it's easy. But because you've already made it through worse."

Word got out.
The letters became a *thing*.

Girls from **Savannah**, **Panama City Beach**, and **St. Augustine** drove hours to read them.

Some even left one of their own.

Chapter 33 –
The Swing Still Squeaks

Laurel found the old tire swing one morning and gave
it a fresh rope.
Janna walked out later that evening to find Laurel
swinging slow, toes barely brushing the grass.

"I used to come out here when I thought nobody
cared," she said.
"Funny thing is… someone always did."

Janna sat beside her in the grass.

"This place… it never stopped loving us. We just had
to come back and let it."

Chapter 34 –
Sunday Mornin' Soft

They started a new tradition — *porch devotions* on Sunday mornings.
No pulpit. No sermon. Just stories, coffee, and that one bluebird who kept landing on the same post.

"You don't need a steeple," Nana Mae said one morning.
"Just a reason to gather."

The barn became a chapel, a safehouse, and a home — all in one breath.

Chapter 35 –
When Sawyer Asked

They were stackin' feed in the back stall when he paused, cleared his throat, and handed her a ring tied to a piece of **bailin' wire**.

"It ain't fancy," he said.
"But neither are we.
What we've got is *real*. You, me, this barn, these people…
Say yes, Janna Rae." She

didn't say a word.

Just kissed him and nodded. And that was all he needed.

Chapter 36 –
Wind in Her Veins

The wedding was held under the pecan trees, with the
barn as the backdrop.
Laurel caught the bouquet. Nana Mae wore boots and
pearls. Janna's dress had lace stitched from her
mama's old church gown.

When the wind blew through her hair during their
vows, Janna smiled.

"Daddy's here," she whispered.
"He's in the wind."

Chapter 37 –
Painted Walls & Open Doors

The barn got a fresh coat of whitewash — not to hide the old, but to honor it.

Kids painted flowers, stars, hearts, and the words:

"You're Safe Here."
"Don't Quit." "Be
Brave."

Every mark was a prayer in color.

Chapter 38 –
The Sound of Laughter Again

Laughter returned to the Calhoun farm.

Real laughter — not polite, not nervous, but the *gutdeep kind* that comes from surviving the storm and finally seeing the sunshine.

They celebrated with bonfires and music.

Even Laurel got up and sang a verse or two.

And Janna?
She stood by Sawyer, heart wide open, arms crossed just like Daddy used to do.

Chapter 39 –
The Barn Knows

One last letter.
Janna wrote it alone, in the loft where she once hid
from the world.

"Dear Barn,"
"You knew the whole time, didn't you?
That healing takes its time. That roots grow slow. That
girls like me — full of fight and fault — would come
back someday and figure it out."

"You didn't save me. But you held me.
And that was enough."

Chapter 40 –
The Light Stays On

Years later, when folks asked where it all started, Janna would just point to the barn.

"That old thing?" she'd say with a wink. "That's where the truth lived."

The Porchlight Project became a haven. A home. A legacy.

But the porchlight?
It never burned out.

It just kept shinin' — **for every soul brave enough to come home.**

Made in the USA
Columbia, SC
23 August 2025

61691458R00063